The Man Who Rode Through Fire

PRAJITH PRABHAKARAN

FanatiXx® Publication
AM/56, Basanti Colony, Rourkela 769012, Odisha
ISO 9001:2015 Certified

By: Prajith Prabhakaran
ISBN: 978-93-5605-666-4
Book: The Man who Rode Through Fire
Price: INR 199/-

Printing By: BooksClub.in

About the Author

Prajith Prabhakaran is a 36-year-old Mechanical Engineer, an IIM Trichy Alumni and a certified API 510, 570, 580, and 653 professional who traded valve stems for handlebar grips and discovered his true calling on two wheels. By day, he ensures the safety of petrochemical plants; by night (and every weekend), he's known online as "ame_riderr," chasing sunrises and mountain passes on his superbike. A seasoned travel vlogger and storyteller, Prajith turned personal triumphs and betrayals into *The Man Who Rode Through Fire*. This memoir novel fuses high-speed adventure with hard-earned life lessons. When he's not racing the dawn or drafting his next chapter, he's planning his next all-India bike ride—and finding inspiration in every curve.

Acknowledgement

Writing *The Man Who Rode Through Fire* has been a journey of grit, growth, and unexpected grace. I owe my deepest thanks to the many people who rode alongside me—through every twist of throttle and every turn of fate.

First and foremost, to Sweta, whose belief in me was the gentlest monsoon after years of drought. Your voice rang truer than any roar of an engine, and your words—"Don't ever turn your back on yourself"—became the beacon that guided me back from the edge. This book is as much yours as it is mine.

To Thajudheen, my brother in helmets and heartbreaks—even when our paths diverged, your early loyalty taught me the cost of trust, and that lesson rippled into these pages.

To Ashiq Sulfikar, fellow author and good friend, thank you for connecting me with the publisher and your unwavering encouragement throughout this process.

To the superbike crew—the friends who polished my ride at midnight, who chased down with me, and who turned every ordinary road into a testament of brotherhood. Your camaraderie fueled every chapter.

To Althaf, Shalil, and all who tested my faith in others: thank you for the fire. Though painful, your betrayals forged the steel of conviction I needed to rebuild—and inspired the heart of this story.

To my family, who weathered countless late-night edits and long rides: your patience and unwavering support reminded me that every journey begins and ends with home.

To my editor, Hemant, whose keen eye and honest feedback transformed my raw memories into a narrative that speaks to both the roar of the engine and the silence of the soul.

To the riding community—online and on the open road—who shared stories, tips, and the simple joy of two wheels and freedom. Your voices echo in every mile I've written.

Finally, to you, the readers: thank you for choosing to ride with me. May these pages remind you that no matter how fierce the flames are, you can emerge stronger, wiser, and ready to lean into the next curve.

Introduction

WHAT YOU WILL DISCOVER IN THIS BOOK & HOW TO GET THE MOST OUT OF READING IT

I was eighteen when I first felt the engine's heartbeat under my fingertips. The dawn was still heavy with night's hush, but my Kawasaki KRR-150 roared to life like a caged thunderstorm released. In that instant, I knew two things with perfect clarity: the road was my sanctuary, and speed—raw, unfiltered speed—was freedom. Every twist of the throttle wiped away yesterday's failures and tomorrow's fears, leaving only the singular pleasure of this moment.

That day marked the beginning of a journey that would blaze through fame and friendship, betrayal and rebirth. I chased horizons painted with sunrise and sunset, believing I could outrun anything life threw at me. I crafted my identity in the mirrors of social media reels, where every lean into the bend, every distant mountain pass, and every mud-spattered off-road plunge became both confession and celebration. My followers numbered in the thousands—and with each new subscriber, the road's quiet solace began to fracture beneath the glare of the spotlight.

Yet beneath every perfect shot lies a story of cuts and bruises—moments no filter can conceal. The adrenaline high of a thousand rides could not shield me from the hollow echo of broken promises. When your world is measured in likes and comments, a single unfollow can resonate louder than the roar of any engine. In chasing speed, I discovered how slow a heartbreak can bleed;

how a friend's betrayal can leave you stranded on an empty highway, headlight dim, heart racing in panic rather than thrill.

But this is not a tale of defeat. It is a testament to the fire itself—how it burns away the dross, how it forges steel from the ashes of ambition and pain.

Fame boasted of loyalty, yet proved no ally when the roads turned rough. I learned that some riders share your passion for the ride… until the first obstacle appears. Brothers in helmets drifted into shadows of doubt; deals I believed would save me nearly destroyed me. The roar of the engine that once sang hope became a relentless reminder of debts unpaid, of trust, misplaced, of the isolation that follows every broken vow.

Amid the wreckage, I found no heroic rescue—only quiet nights haunted by the echo of empty halls and unanswered calls. I faced the bitter realization that life's greatest betrayals often come from those we once called family. Kuruvila's urgent call for help, Jacob's shifting loyalties, and Joseph's broken contracts—all conspired to leave me with nothing but an engine's echo and a vow to survive.

Yet in the deepest darkness, a single spark can ignite a new beginning. I remembered Natasha's voice—gentle as rain, fierce as monsoon winds—echoing in my mind: "Don't turn your back on yourself, Shiva." Her words became the rhythm to which my heart relearned how to beat. I realized that real strength is not shown in flawless runs or seamless climbs but in the courage to lean into the fall, to throttle through the pain, and to keep the ride alive when every part of you wants to abandon the bike for safety.

This book is neither a sermon nor a self-help manual. It is an odyssey of the human spirit dressed in leather and chrome—a chronicle of one man's decision to ride through fire rather than be consumed by it. You will feel the rush of every corner, the sting of every betrayal, and the quiet euphoria of reclaiming your story from the ashes.

Here, you will meet the characters who shaped my fate: the friend whose promise led me into chaos; the brother who turned his back when the road got steep; and the woman whose belief in me became my compass when all other lights went out. You will sit in judgment with me as I navigate courtrooms and cobwebbed memories, and you will share in the reclamation of joy when I discover that freedom has nothing to do with velocity—it has everything to do with truth.

As you turn these pages, imagine the wind on your face, the engine's roar in your chest, and the road stretching out like a white ribbon of hope. Whether you ride two wheels or four, whether your fire is fueled by passion, ambition, or the fight for second chances, know this: the flames that threaten to burn us down can also light the way forward.

So lean in. Grip the bars. And prepare to ride through fire.

Theme

- The joy of love and the pain of irreversible loss
- The healing power of memories and storytelling
- Life on the road vs. stillness in grief
- Crashing dreams and climbing out of them
- Rebuilding self after emotional and physical breakdown
- Faith in the digital age
- The inner life during physical stillness
- Isolation and connection
- The thin line between sanity, divinity and imagination
- Redemption through self-reflection

Main Character

Shiva, 36 a rider and dreamer who loses the love of his life to cancer. As he struggles through business failure and health issues, he finds light again in the one place he never expected... his own story.

A 36-year-old rider and dreamer. Passionate about bikes, freedom, travel. Burned by love, scarred by business failure, and now fighting both physical and emotional wounds. This is his comeback story –told through pain, memory and moments of clarity.

He raced against time, chased dreams across endless highways, and loved with everything he had. But life had a different plan. When the woman he loved passed away from throat cancer, Shiva’s world came crashing down. Love turned into silence, ambition into ashes. A Failed business, a broken body, and nights of unbearable loneliness followed.

But in the stillness of bed rest, he began to write … not to forget her, but to remember everything that burned, and everything that still burns.

The Man Who Rode Through Fire is a powerful, true story of love, loss, healing, and a long ride back to life.

The Man Who Rode Through Fire.

By Prajith Prabhakaran

PART I: THE HEIGHTS (Fame, speed & Social Fire)

1.Spotlight & Speed---Life as an- influencer, full throttle.
2.Flirt Mode On----DMs, attention, and ego on fire.
3.Friends, Fame & Family Feels Good----Surrounded by smiles…for now.
4.Money Like Fuel----Superbikes, supercars, and super confidence.
5.The Message That Changed Everything---A text from Natasha rewrites your story.

PART II: RIDING TOWARD LOVE (Connection & New Dreams)

6.Virtual Sparks----Conversations that feel like destiny.
7.Engine Heat ----New dreams of rides and romance.
8.The Group Crash---Ram Mohan's public insult cuts deep.
9.False Alarms----Shamal, a brother turned backstabber.
10.Calls That Don't Get Answered---2765 contacts.2765 rejections.
11.Memory of promises---Where are those "Anytime bro" people now?
12.Loan Rejections & Lost Hope----Dignity slowly breaks.
13.Natasha's Warmth---Her support becomes your safe space.
14.Tea, Talk & Truth---The first meeting, the first magic.
15.The proposal Without a Ring----Future dreams begin quietly.

PART III: THE FIRE BURNS (Loss, Cancer & Emotional Collapse)

16.A call at Midnight---Her cancer diagnosis stuns you.
17.Prayer & Denial----You fight the truth, and lose.
18.The Last ride----One final moment of love on wheels.
19.Smoke,Not Flame---She's gone. You shatter.
20.The silence After Goodbye---No texts. No calls. Just grief.

PART IV: FALLEN & FORGOTTEN (Loneliness & Reflection)

21.Bedrest Diaries---Your health crashes, forcing you to face your soul.
22.Real Friends, Real Silence---Loyalty disappears in the quiet.
23.The Shadow of My Wall---You're not living, just existing.
24.The Man in the Mirror---Meeting the broken version of you.
25.The Road Ahead---Healing begins with words and wounds.

PART V: BETRAYED IN BUSINESS & BROTHERHOOD

26.Light, Camera, Lie---Film dreams with Jacob begin.
27.Silver Screen, Shattered Trust---The producer shows his real face,
28.Three Years of War---Legal battles, lost hope and time wasted.
29.The Cost of Trust---Friendship broken for money.
30.The Mediator ----Athaf's silence is louder than betrayal.
31.Words Like Blades---Threats, insults, and public humiliation.
32.Silence of Friends---No one stands beside you.
33.Standing Alone ---You hold your head high, even with a broken heart.
34.Metal for Breath---You sell your superbike. Then your car. One by one, your dreams are put on sale---just to pay bills, survive another month, or breathe without guilt.
35.Home on Hold---You mortgage your property. The place that once gave you peace now becomes a burden. But you still keep fighting, not for wealth----but for dignity.

PART VI: THE FINAL BURN & THE REBIRTH

35.Ashes Don't Lie---Everything is gone, except your fire.
36.One More Ride---You ride again. Today, you reclaim your bike ,your car, your home. Not for style---but for closure, for freedom, for her.

Contents

About the Author.......... 3

Acknowledgement.......... 4

Introduction.......... 6

Theme.......... 9

Main Character.......... 10

The Man Who Rode Through Fire.......... 11

Chapter 1:The Rider and the Flame.......... 15

Chapter 2: Vows on Two Wheels.......... 17

Planning the Surprise.......... 17

The Grand Entrance.......... 18

Celebration & Connection.......... 18

A New Beginning.......... 19

Chapter 3: My Promise, Her Legacy.......... 23

Chapter 4: The King of the Fast Lane.......... 28

Chapter 5: Mansoor's Entry – The Storm on the Track.......... 31

Chapter 6: Rivalry to Brotherhood – Rise of the Underdog.......... 33

Chapter 7: The Message That Burned It All.......... 35

Chapter 8: Spotlight & Speed.......... 38

Chapter 9: Flirt Mode On.......... 41

Chapter 10: Friends, Fame & Family Feels Good.......... 44

Chapter 11: Money Like Fuel.......... 47

Chapter 12: The Message That Changed Everything.......... 50

Chapter 13: Origin of Ame Rider.......... 53

Chapter 14: Virtual Sparks.......... 55

Chapter 15: Engine Heat 58
Chapter 16: The Group Crash 60
Chapter 17: False Alarms 63
Chapter 18: Calls That Don't Get Answered 66
Chapter 19: Memory of Promises 69
Chapter 20: Loan Rejections & Lost Hope 72
Chapter 21: Natasha's Warmth 75
Chapter 22: Tea, Talk & Truth 78
Chapter 23: The Proposal Without a Ring 81
Chapter 24: A Call at Midnight 84
Chapter 25: Prayer & Denial 88
Chapter 26: The Last Ride 91
Chapter 27: Smoke, Not Flame 95
Chapter 28: The Silence After Goodbye 98
Chapter 29: Bedrest Diaries 101
Chapter 30: Real Friends, Real Silence 105
Chapter 31: The Shadow on My Wall 108
Chapter 32: The Man in the Mirror 111
Chapter 33: The Road Ahead 114
Chapter 34: The Call That Changed Nothing 117
Chapter 35: Truth in Black and White 120
Chapter 36: Born of Ash 122
Chapter 37: Ashes Don't Lie 124
Chapter 38: Fire Doesn't Destroy, It Reveals 126
Chapter 39: Truth in Black and White 128
Chapter 40: The Last Flame Falls 130

Chapter 1: The Rider and the Flame

The road stretched like a dark ribbon beneath the twilight sky. The engine's growl echoed through the silence as I pulled my superbike to a stop on a quiet hilltop. I switched off the ignition. Just me, my machine, and the wind whispering stories of the past.

Before all this—the pain, the fall, the silence—I was the man everyone wanted to be. Influencer. Entrepreneur. Racer. The one with supercars, superbikes, brand deals, and followers who cheered for every move I made. My phone buzzed every minute. My inbox overflowed with offers. Friends, relatives, even people who once doubted me—everyone wanted to stand close when the spotlight was on.

But flames don't only light up a stage. Sometimes, they burn everything you love.

My journey didn't begin with pain. It began with speed. With the rush of the throttle, the blur of lights, the freedom of the open road. Riding wasn't just my passion—it was my therapy, my rebellion, my language. I rode not to escape life, but to embrace it.

And then one day, a message changed everything.

"Hi… I saw your superbike post. I was wondering… can you help me with a ride to my brother's wedding? He loves bikes, and I want to surprise him."

That was the first message from ****Natasha****—the woman who would later become the most beautiful part of my story… and the deepest scar on my heart.

At first, it felt like just another message from a follower. I'd received hundreds like it—people asking for collaborations, fans wanting a ride, brands looking to pitch. But something about her words stood out. Maybe it was her tone—gentle, warm, respectful. Or maybe, deep inside, something told me this wasn't going to be just a ride.

We chatted. She introduced herself. Natasha. A girl with a soft voice and a strong soul. She wasn't trying to impress me. She was real. Honest. In a world full of filters, her simplicity struck me like thunder in a silent sky.

Chapter 2: Vows on Two Wheels

The morning of Kiran's wedding dawned bright and warm. Natasha caught me in the hallway, excitement lighting her eyes like neon. "Shiva," she whispered, "Kiran's begged me—his big day won't be the same without your superbike in the procession. He loves it more than anything."

I nodded, heart thudding. I'd promised her brother a ride, but Natasha wanted more: a grand entrance, a memory that would last forever. I had exactly twenty-four hours to turn this wedding into a roar of engines and a blaze of joy.

Planning the Surprise

That evening, I met the crew at our usual haunt—the half-lit garage by the highway. Five riders, five bikes polished to a mirror shine. I laid out the plan:

1. Arrival Formation: We'd ride in staggered V-shape, engine thunder echoing through the wedding grounds just as the baraat procession reached the mandap.
2. Decor & Presentation: Each bike would carry garlands of marigold and spray-painted "Team Fire" decals. At the front, my blue superbike would bear a ribbon like a bridal gift.
3. Gift Reveal: After circling the groom's car, we'd pull up, hand Kiran a customized riding helmet engraved with his name—and then mount up for a celebratory lap around the venue lawn.

The team cheered. Helmets snapped on. We spent the night under the glow of work lights, weaving flowers through handlebars, testing revs, and practising our synchronized pull-ups.

The Grand Entrance

The wedding pavilion buzzed with relatives and dancers when our moment came. A hush fell as the baraat—Kiran in sherwani, turban pristine—approached the mandap in a decorated car. Just as the dhol players reached their crescendo, we cut our engines to silence … and then unleashed a thunderous roar that rippled through the courtyard.

Natasha's gasp was louder than any drum. Guests turned, laughter and awe mixing in the air. My blue superbike led the formation, ribbons fluttering. We wound our way between guests, perfectly timed, circling Kiran's car three times before coming to a halt.

I swung down and approached him, helmet in hand. His eyes widened as I untied the ribbon and lifted the visor—there, in silver script, was "Ride Safe, Kiran". He pressed the helmet to his chest, voice thick:

"Shiva… you made this day epic."

He put it on, settling it snugly, and we both laughed—the kind of laughter that felt like home.

Celebration & Connection

As the ceremony resumed, we joined the post-vows celebration. The team lined up our bikes under the fairy lights; petals rained from balconies. Natasha found me among the crowd, her smile softer now, her eyes reflecting the twinkle of lamps.

"Thank you," she said, touching my arm. "You outdid yourself."

We danced to the upbeat tempo of the wedding band—me on my feet, Natasha beside me. For a moment, I forgot every betrayal, every lonely ride. All that mattered was her hand in mine, the warmth of the night, and the roar of friendship in every engine.

During the feast, Kiran raised a toast:

"To my sister, and to the man who rides through fire for us."

Glasses clinked. Natasha's face turned toward me, pride and something softer shining there.

A New Beginning

Later, as the last guests drifted away and the bikes lined up under the moonlight, Natasha slipped her arm through mine. "You made him happier than I've ever seen," she whispered. "And you reminded me why I believed in you."

I looked at her—so vibrant, so real—and felt something shift. The ride that began with engines and adrenaline had led me here, to a quiet truth: that love and loyalty can roar just as loudly as any superbike.

We climbed onto our bikes together for one final lap around the lawn, Natasha's laughter trailing behind us like a melody. Under the stars, I realized that this surprise wasn't just for Kiran—it was for us both.

And as the engines faded into the night, I knew our journey was only just beginning.

The morning sun painted the ancestral mansion in soft rose gold as we arrived on the sprawling grounds, Shiva at the helm of his blue superbike and Natasha guiding her brother, Kiran, by the hand. The air hummed with excitement and distant temple bells, carrying the promise of a day that would be remembered for generations.

Natasha's family home—an elegant blend of colonial architecture and traditional Kerala motifs—stood at the heart of a verdant courtyard. Mango and jackfruit trees formed a canopy over polished laterite stone paths. Every surface gleamed: the carved wooden doors, the brass lamps lining the walkways, and even the courtyard's lotus-filled pond reflected the sky like liquid sapphire.

As we dismounted, a line of elders in pristine white mundus and silk saris greeted us with garlands of jasmine. Their smiles were warm and genuine—an embodiment of the kindness I had come to cherish in Natasha's family. She introduced me with a proud sparkle in her eyes: "This is Shiva, the one who always rides through fire for us."

We followed her into the main pavilion, where a chorus of drummers played a celebratory beat. The hall was lined with rows of chairs draped in ivory cloth, and at the far end, the mandap stood magnificent under a canopy of marigolds and banana leaves. But beyond the ceremonial stage, my gaze drew to the scenes unfolding on either side.

On one wing of the grounds, fifty simple weddings were taking place simultaneously. Beautiful brides in crimson and gold sat beside grooms in crisp dhotis, each couple framed by a modest canopy of banana stalks and coconut fronds. These were the fifty unions Natasha's father had pledged to sponsor—for families who could never have afforded a wedding feast. Thai Pongal pots bubbled gently over small fires, and artists wove garlands from temple flowers for every bride and groom. As I watched tears of joy sparkle in the bride's eyes, I felt the weight of this generosity settle in my chest—a lesson in compassion more powerful than any ride.

On the other wing, tiered stainless-steel platters groaned under the weight of twenty thousand meals. Volunteers ladled rice and sambar in perfect synchronization, while servers offered piping-hot payasam from gleaming brass urns. Families from nearby villages moved through the serving lines with gratitude so profound it lent each plate a sacred quality.

At the centre of it, all was Natasha's father, Mahadevan Pillai—a man whose lineage traced back centuries, whose family wealth was rivalled by none in Kerala. Yet he moved among the crowds with effortless humility, greeting everyone by name, inquiring about their children's health, including labourers and priests with the same respectful nod. He wore simple white kurtas, his silver hair braided neatly at the nape, his eyes shining with the quiet contentment of one who knows that true wealth is measured in lives uplifted.

Natasha and I made our way to the mandap as Kiran, resplendent in his sherwani, approached on a decorated elephant—another token of the family's love for Kerala's heritage. The elephant's forehead was painted in sacred patterns, its bells chiming softly with each step. Guests rose to their feet, applause rippling through the courtyard like sunlit waves.

When the ceremonial vows began, the air seemed to be still. Sacred chants from the Vedic priests rose in harmony with the temple bells, crafting a soundtrack that was both ancient and alive. I watched Kiran slip the mangalsutra around his bride's neck, and as he did, I saw in Natasha's eyes a profound pride—and a hint of wistfulness for days gone by.

After the rites, Natasha led me through a side corridor lined with family portraits—generations of Pillais in crisp mundus and gold-bordered saris, each couple's union commemorated in sepia-toned photographs. She paused before a black-and-white image of her great-grandparents, who had founded this estate. "They believed," she whispered, "that our duty was to honour our blessings by sharing them. Every generation since has upheld that promise."

I slipped an arm around her waist, feeling the warmth of her confidence in her roots. At that moment, surrounded by decades of legacy and the laughter of fifty new couples, I understood that her strength—the same strength that once washed over me like a monsoon—was born from this very tradition of giving.

As the evening lanterns flickered to life and the smell of incense mingled with freshly cooked payasam, I realized that this grand celebration was more than a wedding. It was a testament to the power of family, the grace of generosity, and the truth that even the richest inheritances are measured by the hearts they touch.

And for Natasha and me, in this kaleidoscope of vows and blessings, our own story found its next chapter. A chapter bound by heritage, elevated by love and destined to ride forward—together—through whatever fires lay ahead.

Chapter 3: My Promise, Her Legacy

Days turned into weeks. The wedding came and went. Her brother got his superbike moment, and I got something I hadn't expected—*peace*. Talking to her felt like parking my soul after years of running on empty. And then... we unexpectedly matched on a matrimony site. Fate was now laughing in my face, writing our story line by line.

Meanwhile, I was riding high. Business was booming. My brand was growing. I had fans in millions, a life many envied. I bought what I loved—machines that roared, tyres that burned, roads that obeyed only me. And along with me, my circle expanded. Friends, cousins, advisors, "well-wishers"—all clapping as long as my wallet and smile were full.

But success is a dangerous drug. It blinds you. And I never saw the storm coming.

One day, I received a message in a WhatsApp group. Ram Mohan—a name I had respected—insulted me publicly. Called me a fraud in recruitment. Said I was playing with people's lives. A single message, broadcasted to a group of professionals, ruined years of credibility. Just like that.

I laughed it off—at first. I thought, "Let him bark. I'll ride past this." But that message… it started a fire.

The fire spread fast. Shamal, one of my closest friends—someone who had shared my dreams, my nights, my rides—spread the news that my business had collapsed. He didn't even ask. Didn't check in. Just added fuel to gossip. And suddenly, I wasn't the rider anymore—I was the wreck.

I turned to people. 2,765 contacts on my phone. Each one had once said, "Bro, anything you need, just ask."

So I asked. One by one. For help. For a loan. For support. All I got back was silence.

The same people who clapped when I bought my superbike disappeared when I had to sell it. The ones who came to my housewarming were nowhere when I pledged my property to the bank. My shadow, and my heartbeat, were my only companions.

And through all this… Natasha stayed. She messaged. She encouraged. She believed in me when I had stopped believing in myself.

But life… doesn't let you rest in peace, even when you're still breathing.

While the world walked away, **Natasha walked in.** Every morning, a message from her. Not grand speeches, not fake motivation—just truth. Some days it was a "How are you holding up?" Other days, "Don't give up. I'm here." In those messages, I found something rare—*care without condition*.

We started talking more. About life, struggles, and dreams. She told me about her past, her pain, her little victories. And I opened up too—for the first time, fully. No filters. No branding. No show.

We were strangers once, but now… she had my heart. And without asking, I knew I had hers.

At the same time, my world was burning.

The movie investment with **Jacob**—one of my oldest friends—turned into a nightmare. We had trusted a producer, and gave him financial backing, hoping to support his vision and earn returns. But three years passed, and all we got back was excuses, lies, and finally—just the capital, without a single rupee of profit.

There were **fights**, **legal threats**, **sleepless nights**. The producer humiliated me, used filthy language, and threatened me like I was the one who owed him. The person who introduced me to that deal, **Kuruvila**, tried to act as a middleman, but by then, the damage was already done.

I wasn't just losing money—I was losing pieces of myself.

My bike—gone.

My cars—gone.

My dreams—crushed. Even my **house**, my **property**, I pledged to the bank—just to breathe through the storm.

And yet, every evening, I would sit by my window, stare at the road, and imagine the throttle in my hand again. Not because I needed speed, but because I needed to feel *alive*.

And then… just when I thought things couldn't break me more, came the blow I never saw coming.

Natasha stopped messaging. One day. Two days. A week. Nothing. My heart raced faster than any superbike I had ever ridden. I tried calling. No answer. I messaged. No reply.

Finally, her brother called me.

His voice was shaking. “She’s gone, Shiva…”

Stage two throat cancer. Diagnosed late. Fought silently. And she didn’t want me to worry.

She left without a goodbye.

I remember falling to the floor. Not like in movies. No dramatic screams. Just quiet. Just me and the echo of everything I had lost.

The room was silent, but my heart screamed.

I sat there, on the cold floor, holding my phone with trembling hands. I scrolled through her messages, rereading every word, every emoji, every “Take care” and “Don’t give up.”

She knew.

She knew she was running out of time, yet never let it slip. She gave me strength while hiding her own war. That was Natasha—*my angel with a ticking clock.*

In those moments, something inside me shattered… but something else began to burn.

Grief didn’t knock. It broke the door. I stopped eating. Stopped answering calls. I became a ghost inside my own home. And every time I looked in the mirror, I saw a stranger—a man who once rode with fire in his soul, now crushed beneath the ashes.

But here’s what life forgot—I am not built to stay broken.

One night, I stood on the same hilltop where this story began. I looked at the city lights below and whispered, *“Natasha… if you’re listening, I’ll rise again. I’ll ride again. For you.”*

That was the promise.

The next morning, I opened my notebook. Not a business plan. Not a to-do list. But words—my words, my pain, my truth.

This book. This is not just my comeback. This is her legacy. This is for every man who lost everything, for every rider who ran out of road, for every lover who was left with silence.

I'm not the man I used to be. I'm not the influencer, the entrepreneur, or the boy with big machines. **I am the man who rode through fire. And lived.**

Chapter 4: The King of the Fast Lane

Before heartbreak.

Before humiliation.

Before the silence…

There was **speed.**

There was **success.**

There was *me*—living a life many only dreamed of.

I was 30, bold, and burning with ambition. My phone was an extension of my brand. Instagram was my stage. Every reel, every post, every ride—was met with hearts, shares, and applause. People followed not just for the bikes, but for the vibe. The energy. The *attitude*.

And yeah, I flirted. A lot.

DMs weren't just for networking—they were buzzing with fans, followers, and curious strangers. Some were genuine, some fake. But I was in control. I didn't chase love. I rode past it. Fast. That was my style.

I had it all.

Superbikes that roared like thunder. **Supercars that painted streets with envy.** **Parties that lit up the night.** **Followers in thousands, admirers in silence.**

I wasn't just an influencer—I was an entrepreneur with a fireproof vision. Recruitment, brand collaborations, digital consulting—I turned my passions into profit. And every success story had my name somewhere in the credits.

Friends? I had plenty.

They raised glasses when I bought my first Ducati.

They clapped the loudest when I crossed 100k followers.

They posted selfies outside my house like they belonged there.

They said, "Bro, you're next level. Whatever you need—just ask."

But I never asked. Because when you're on top, you don't expect to fall.

And I was soaring.

My father smiled proudly.

My mother lit lamps for me every day.

Relatives who once doubted me now quoted me.

Cousins copied my captions.

Life was loud, rich, and fast. But what no one saw was the price I paid:

Sleepless nights.

Endless hustle.

Loneliness hidden behind likes.

Fake friends disguised as fans.

But I didn't care. As long as I had the road, the throttle, and my fire—I was invincible.

Until one day… the cracks started to show.

And what began with whispers… ended in an explosion.

Chapter 5: Mansoor's Entry – The Storm on the Track

I still remember the first time I saw Mansoor.

It was at a district-level racing event in Kerala—the kind where the roar of engines drowns out everything else and legends are whispered long before the first flag drops. His name echoed through the crowd even before the engines started. Everyone knew who he was. A storm on two wheels.

To me, he was an opponent. A threat. The unbeatable champion, known for his ruthless precision and fearless throttle control. He didn't talk much. Just rode like a storm—and won like a king.

We were rivals from the very first race. I wanted to beat him. I had to beat him—not just for the trophy, but for the validation. But to him, I was probably just another name on the race list.

Still, every time I raced him, something began to change. He started noticing me—not for what I was, but for what I could be. Maybe he saw a reflection of himself in me—raw fire, wild energy, untamed spirit.

After a close finish one day, when I nearly caught up with him, he walked up to me—not with arrogance, but with calm respect.

"You've got something," he said. "But you're missing the edge. You ride with heart, but not with clarity."

I didn't know whether to feel insulted or honoured. But what he said next hit me like a punch to the soul:

"Come train with me."

That moment changed everything.

I soon learned that Mansoor wasn't just a racer—he was a Commander in the Indian Army. His discipline was military-grade. His life was a balance between defending the nation and dancing with danger on the racetrack.

Weekends and off-duty hours became our battlefield. He taught me things no book or video could:

- Racing lines
- Cornering posture
- Throttle and braking balance
- Reading the track like a soldier reads terrain

But above all, he taught me mentality.

To ride without fear.

To respect the machine.

To find silence in chaos.

To control fire without letting it consume you.

Mansoor—the man I once saw as my biggest threat—became my mentor. My fire. My brother.

Racing gave me speed.

**Mansoor gave me direction. **

Chapter 6: Rivalry to Brotherhood – Rise of the Underdog

Under Mansoor's guidance, I wasn't the same rider anymore.

I wasn't chasing podiums—I was chasing purpose.

Every time I zipped up my racing jacket, something within me shifted. The fear that once shadowed me before a race vanished. Now, there was only focus. Silence. Flame.

People began to notice.

The same racers who once mocked my presence now nodded in quiet respect. The underdog was no longer just participating—he was winning. I started winning local races—first district, then state level.

But with every victory, I never forgot the journey.

The humiliations,

The nights I cried silently,

The betrayals,

The moments I almost gave up.

And through it all—Mansoor was there. Watching from the sidelines. No claps. No speeches. Just that quiet, proud smile. The look of a brother who had believed in me before I believed in myself.

He taught me to ride like a warrior—but more than that, he taught me to live like one.

To race not for attention, but for truth.

To ride not with ego, but with honor.

To transform pain into power.

Off the track, people began to ask:

- "How did you do it?"
- "What changed?"

They thought it was the bike. Or maybe the gear. Or the technique.

But I knew the truth.
It wasn't just petrol that fueled me.
It was pain.
It was brotherhood.
It was belief.

This wasn't just my victory.

It was the victory of every underdog who was ever told they weren't enough.

Every dreamer who raced against doubt.

Every soul who chose to rise—even when it hurt.

Because in the fire of racing, I found myself.

And in Mansoor, I found a brother.

Chapter 7: The Message That Burned It All

It began like any other day.

Coffee. Emails. A few reels on Instagram. A ride was planned for the evening.

Then—*ping*.

A WhatsApp notification. One of my professional groups. A space where opportunities were shared and respect was mutual.

But this time, it wasn't a request for help or a thank-you message.

It was an *attack*.

From Ram Mohan.

Someone I had known for years—not just from work or industry circles, but from our *college days*. We sat in the same classrooms. Shared the same canteen benches. Walked across the same campus as engineering graduates.

But while I fought hard to build my career—through sweat, sleepless nights, and sacrifice—Ram Mohan took shortcuts.

He didn't even clear his 19 back papers. Instead of completing his degree honestly, he *bought a fake certificate* from an agency.

He couldn't walk the road I did, so he tried to block mine. And now, years later, this same man who once came to me for advice… was labelling me as a fraud in front of hundreds.

"Be careful of this guy. He's running fake recruitment. Don't trust him."

The message stung. But the *hypocrisy?* That was poison.

No one paused to ask me the truth. They just watched—like spectators at a public hanging.

And the deeper wound came from someone even closer—**Shamal.**

He wasn't just a friend. He was handling all my **vehicle-related businesses**. He had keys to my dreams—my cars, my bikes, my legacy.

But in my downfall, he didn't stand by me. **He added fuel to the fire.**

"Shiva's business is cracked, bro. Nothing's left." And then the punchline, his favourite joke—

"Only one thing's not cracked... his firecrackers business!"

Laughter followed. I heard it. Someone even forwarded the voice note to me.

They laughed like I was some circus act.

The same people who once celebrated my wins now celebrate my ruin.

But here's the truth they didn't know:

I didn't fall because I was weak. I fell because I was **carrying too much**—dreams, debts, trust, and the weight of other people's expectations.

And still, even in my silence, **I burned. ** Quietly. Fiercely. Alone.

Chapter 8: Spotlight & Speed

The day I crossed the finish line and held that first-state-level trophy in my hands, something shifted. Not just in me—but around me.

I uploaded a short reel—15 seconds.

Me.

Thc bike.

The win.

A slow-mo burnout with the caption:

“Earned. Not Given.”

That one video exploded.

Shares. Comments. DMs.

Thousands of people started following.

Not because I was rich.

Not because I was famous.

Because I had done what so many were scared to do:

Start again. From nothing.

My inbox overflowed with questions about bikes, gear, racing, and life. Strangers treated me like a celebrity. Friends who once ignored me started reposting my stories.

And I?

I kept riding.

Every weekend became a stage.

Every ride—content.

Every smile from a stranger—fuel.

I was addicted. Not to attention… but to earn it.

Soon, the collabs started coming in.

Gear brands, energy drinks, bike dealers…

Money started to flow—not like a flood, but like a steady stream.

Enough to fix some broken dreams. Enough to start building again.

I bought a new camera. Hired a friend to shoot my rides. Launched a YouTube channel.

Subscribers? 0.

Views? 3.

But passion? Limitless.

That phase of my life was wild.

Superbikes. Super followers. Super confidence.

I wasn't just a rider anymore—I was a brand.

People wanted to ride with me. Talk like me. Post like me.

And for a while…

It felt like I had it all.

But fame is a funny thing.

It's not always a reward.

Sometimes, it's a test.

Little did I know…

The real fire hadn't even started yet.

Chapter 9: Flirt Mode On

Before the reels, before the attention, before the ego… there was Devika.

She was my first real dream—not of bikes or fame—but of love.

From childhood, I saw her not just as a girl, but as my future.

I didn't chase her like boys did in school.

I made her a promise.

"Once I finish my studies and have a stable job, I'll come to your home—with my head held high—to ask for your hand."

I meant it.

Every late-night study session, every job interview, every extra shift I worked—it wasn't just for success.

It was for her.

So I could stand tall in front of her parents and say,

"I'm ready. I'm the man who kept his word."

And finally, when that day came—when I had the job, the respect, the dreams—I went looking for her.

What I found broke me in ways even high-speed crashes never could.

She wasn't waiting.

She had moved on.

With her college classmate.

And I didn't just hear about it—I saw it.

With my own eyes.

A moment that shattered the years I carried silently inside me.

The promises.

The discipline.

The sacrifices.

They meant nothing to her.

That night, something inside me snapped—not in anger, but in cold silence.

"Why should I wait? Why should I believe in forever, when forever was broken like it never mattered?"

And just like that…

My heart turned off.

And the flirt mode turned on.

Not because I loved the attention.

Not because I wanted to play.

But because I had trusted too deeply—and was left with nothing.

The DMs became my escape.

The jokes, the smooth lines, the late-night chats—they weren't about love.

They were about distraction.

People saw the confident, charming rider.

No one saw the broken boy behind the helmet.

That chapter wasn't about lust.

It was about loss.

And trying to feel something again—even if it was fake.

Devika never knew the fire she lit.

Not the good one.

Not the one that burned everything inside me.

Chapter 10: Friends, Fame & Family Feels Good

(Rise in the riding world, social media growth, adrenaline, and the early sparks of public recognition.)

Life has a strange way of balancing pain with applause.

While my heart quietly stitched itself back together, the world outside clapped louder than ever.

The fame, the reels, the rides—they brought me a different kind of love.

People who once doubted me now send me voice notes asking for tips on bikes, cameras, and followers.

I was being called to host events, lead rides, and talk about my "journey to success"—as if it had always been sunshine and smooth roads.

But no one knew the fuel was heartbreak.

Still, for a while, it felt good.

Friends surrounded me like a pack.

We rode in formation, engines roaring through the streets like we owned the night.

Photoshoots. Café meetups. Night rides.

It all looked like a movie.

And my family?

They finally smiled when they looked at me.

After all the silence, rejection, and confusion, they saw me rising.

My mother started saving my newspaper cuttings.

My dad, who once warned me to focus on a "safe life," now shares my YouTube videos with relatives.

"Look at my son," he'd say.

"He made it his way."

Their pride gave me peace.

For the first time in years, I walked into my home not as a question mark—but as an answer.

But here's the truth most people won't admit:

Fame feels good.

Family pride feels even better.

But the pain never fully leaves. It just hides behind filters and fast rides.

Behind every group photo was a piece of me still searching…

For something real.

For someone true.

For silence that felt like home.

But I smiled anyway.

Because sometimes, that’s what survivors do.

They turn the fire into a show.

Chapter 11: Money Like Fuel

Money.

That thing I once begged banks for…

Now it started coming in from places I never expected.

Instagram collabs.

YouTube monetization.

Paid ride appearances.

Merch sales.

Brands sending gear with "Bro just tag us once" written in the DMs.

Suddenly, I wasn't counting rupees for petrol—I was calculating ROI for every reel.

And damn, the power felt addictive.

I remember the day I walked into the showroom and booked the superbike I used to only dream of. No co-signer. No fear.

Just a confident:

"Full cash. Deliver it before Sunday."

The salesman who once ignored me during my broke days?

He offered me tea this time. Smiled wide. Called me "sir."

I didn't forget that face.

The supercar came next—not new, but enough to turn heads at signals.

I'd stop at a red light, and phones would point at me like I was some movie star.

Some would ask:

"Which film are you in, bro?"

I'd smile and think:

This is the film. My life is the damn movie.

But here's the twist:

The more I earned, the less impressed I was.

With money.

With people.

Even with myself.

Because deep down, I knew where this all began.

Not with a brand deal.

Not with a trend.

But with pain.

With a broken promise.

With Devika. With Natasha. With the nights I slept hugging failure like a blanket.

Money became my fuel, yes.

It helped me travel. Breathe easier. Feel powerful.

But it also made me realize…

Fuel burns.

And if you're not careful, it burns you too.

So I learned to ride smarter.

Not just on the road—but in life.

I wasn't chasing luxuries anymore.

I was chasing peace.

But the world still saw the shine.

The chrome.

The throttle.

The flex.

And I let them.

Because not everyone needs to know the full story.

Some flames are meant to be felt, not explained.

Chapter 12: The Message That Changed Everything

Where fire meets calm, and one message touches a place nothing else could reach.

It was a normal night.

Another late scroll through notifications, DMs, meaningless replies, and fake emojis. I wasn't looking for anything. Just killing time between reels and real life.

And then, her message appeared.

Natasha.

Not a follower. Not a fangirl.

Just… someone who saw me.

Her first message didn't say "Nice bike" or "Big fan."

She wrote:

"Your eyes in that last reel looked tired. Are you okay?"

I froze.

Thousands had reacted to the post.

Hundreds commented on the engine, the stunt, and the background music.

But only one person saw past the helmet.

I didn't know how to respond.

It had been so long since someone asked how I really was.

That night, we talked for hours.

Not about bikes or fame.

But about life. Regret. Dreams. Silence. Loss.

And somehow, with every reply, I felt my walls slowly cracking.

She wasn't trying to fix me.

She was just there.

Listening. Understanding. Being.

Days turned into weeks.

Voice notes became routine.

Mornings started with her good morning texts.

Nights ended with her voice saying,

"You did well today."

It felt like riding at 300 km/h and finally finding a smooth straight road.

No speed breakers.

No potholes.

Just peace.

Natasha didn't come into my life like a storm.

She came in like rain after the fire.

And with just one message…

She reminded me of something I had forgotten:

I am still capable of being loved.

Genuinely.

Quietly.

Without filters.

That message didn't just change my day.

It changed the direction of my life.

Chapter 13: Origin of Ame Rider

Natasha's words fell soft and sudden—like the first drop of monsoon on parched earth—when she called you "Ame Rider." In her tongue, ame means rain: each syllable a cool whisper against fevered skin.

By naming you "rain," she invites these images:

- Cleansing: You sweep away the dust of yesterday's betrayals, leaving every road you ride fresh and bright, like streets washed clean by a sudden shower.
- Renewal: Just as rain coaxes buds and blooms from cracked earth, your presence awakens hope in her heart—sprouting dreams she thought long dead.
- Rhythm and Flow: Rain doesn't roar—it drips, it pitter-patters, it dances on rooftops. So does your journey: every twist, every turn, every rev of the engine falls into its own natural cadence.
- Unpredictable Grace: Sometimes gentle, sometimes fierce, rain arrives on its own terms. Like you, it cannot be tamed—only embraced, respected, loved.

In calling you Ame Rider, Natasha baptizes you in her most tender metaphor: you are both storm and sanctuary, an ever-moving downpour of possibility, carrying her away from drought into the lush promise of every road ahead.

And with just one message…

She reminded me of something I had forgotten:

I am still capable of being loved.

Genuinely.

Quietly.

Without filters.

That message didn't just change my day.

It changed the direction of my life.

Chapter 14: Virtual Sparks

With Natasha, it wasn't fireworks—it was a slow, steady flame that felt… safe.

Every message, every late-night voice note, every inside joke—built something I hadn't felt in years:

Trust.

She wasn't impressed by my followers or the bike I rode.

She wanted to know what kept me awake at night, not what kept my Instagram running.

We'd talk about things others never stayed long enough to ask about.

My dreams, my past failures, the girl I once waited for, the brotherhood that betrayed me.

And she?

She opened up too.

Not with drama, but with vulnerability.

We talked about broken families.

Pressure.

Loneliness.

The kind of pain you carry with a smile.

There were moments—between texts and voice calls—where silence wasn't awkward.

It was healing.

I remember one night, she said:

"I don't know why, but it feels like I've known you forever."

And I replied without thinking:

"Maybe in another life, we didn't get enough time."

The spark was lit.

We hadn't met yet.

No dates.

No selfies.

Just energy.

Raw. Real. Unfiltered.

I started sleeping better.

Eating better.

Even riding differently—more mindfully, like I had something to protect.

Someone to ride toward, not just away from my past.

For the first time since I lost Natasha,

since I was betrayed,

since I flirted to forget—

I wasn't escaping.

I was arriving.

And all it took…

was connected without pressure.

Vulnerability without judgment.

Two souls sharing scars instead of showing off trophies.

This wasn't love yet.

But it was the kind of spark that could survive storms.

And I, the man who rode through the fire,

was finally warming his hands with something real.

Chapter 15: Engine Heat

The first time she heard the engine roar through a voice note, she laughed.

“Your bike sounds like it’s growling at me,” she joked.

I replied,

“It’s jealous. You’re getting more attention than it does.”

Natasha was different.

She didn’t just listen to my rides—she asked about them.

Why this model? Why this exhaust? What does riding feel like?

And when I told her…

“It’s not the speed. It’s the silence I find inside it,”

she didn’t laugh.

She understood.

Soon, the rides weren’t just for content or clout.

They became dedications.

I’d stop mid-ride to record the sunset for her.

Send her the sounds of the wind when I crossed 200 km/h, just because she once said it felt “like freedom through the phone.”

Every ride had a destination now—even if it was just the next voice note to her.

And slowly, new dreams started forming.

Not just about the next bike or the next milestone.

But dreams where she was in the backseat, holding me.

Dreams of two helmets on one mirror.

Of pitstops filled with chai and long talks.

Of touring places not for reels—but for memories.

One night, she said,

"I want to learn to ride one day. But only if you teach me."

I stared at that message longer than I'd admit.

Because in that moment, I saw a future I wasn't sure I'd ever believe in again.

One where love and passion didn't compete.

They coexisted.

The fire in my life had always been fast, fierce, and burning.

But with her, the engine heat felt different—warm, not wild.

I wasn't racing anymore.

I was riding towards something.

Or maybe… someone.

Chapter 16: The Group Crash

It was supposed to be just another weekend ride.

A group ride with the usual boys—leather jackets, GoPros, and fake loyalty.

We'd done this a hundred times before.

Same roads. Same bikes. The same ego battles are masked as "friendly competition."

But that day, something felt off.

Maybe it was the way Ram Mohan was riding—more aggressive than usual.

Or the way he looked at me before we rolled out—like a challenge, not a brother.

I didn't think much of it.

Until the café stop.

We parked up, all eyes on us like always.

Someone asked who led the pack, and who clocked the highest speed.

And just like that, Ram Mohan stood up and laughed—loud, mocking, heavy.

"Bro, this guy? Shiva? He's all reels and drama. Real riders know who leads."

The silence that followed…

wasn't just awkward.

It was humiliating.

Laughter from the group.

Whispers behind sunglasses.

Phones out, catching reactions.

My heart was calm—but my pride?

Shattered.

This wasn't a stranger.

This was someone I'd helped, supported, and rode beside.

And now?

He threw me under the bus just for a few claps and clout.

I looked around—no one stood up for me.

Not one so-called "brother" said a word.

I stood alone. Again.

I didn't argue.

I didn't explode.

I just quietly picked up my helmet…

and left.

The ride back home felt longer than usual.

Not because of the distance—

but because something inside me broke that day.

The illusion of brotherhood.

The fake cheers.

The surface-level support.

After that day, I started riding solo more.

Not out of anger—but out of truth.

Because when the crash comes—real or emotional—you find out who's really riding with you.

And most people?

They just want to follow…

until they feel like overtaking.

Chapter 17: False Alarms

If Ram Mohan's insult was loud and public,

Shamal's betrayal was silent and sharp—like a knife slid gently between the ribs.

This was different.

Shamal wasn't just a riding buddy.

He was my brother—not by blood, but by belief.

The kind of guy you call when your tyre bursts at midnight.

The one who knew my family, my struggles, my heartbreaks.

We'd built dreams together.

Talked about starting a moto-vlog channel.

Launching a biker cafe.

Even planned a ride to Leh that we never took—but swore we would.

And then came the silence.

First, it was the delayed replies.

Then ignored calls.

Then excuses that didn't sound like him.

At first, I thought—he's busy.

Life gets hectic. Maybe he's overwhelmed.

But then I heard it.

Through a mutual friend, I found out he had started the same vlog idea we built together—with another crew.

Not a word to me.

Not even a heads-up.

He used our name.

Our tagline.

Our ride plans.

And when I finally called him out?

"Bro, it's not like you owned the idea. I just moved forward. You were too emotional, man."

Too emotional.

That's what he called my loyalty.

My friendship.

My belief in brotherhood.

It wasn't even the project that hurt.

It was the way he made me feel—like I was replaceable.

All those late-night dreams.

The support during hard times.

The belief that some people would never leave?

False alarms.

Warnings I ignored.

Red flags I chose not to see because I loved him like family.

But he rang the bell and walked away before the fire even started.

That day, I learned:

Not all betrayals are loud.

Some come dressed in silence, wearing your old memories like a mask.

And once again, I stood in the ashes.

Not because I fell—

But because someone I trusted chose to burn the bridge.

Chapter 18: Calls That Don't Get Answered

Rock bottom isn't a place.

It's a ringtone that never gets picked up.

After Shamal vanished, and Ram Mohan embarrassed me,

things started spiralling.

A business deal collapsed.

An EMI bounced.

And I—the man with the reels, the rides, the respect—was back to staring at my bank balance and wondering how I'd make it through the next month.

So I did what most people do when their world starts shaking—I reached out.

One by one, I opened my contact list.

2765 contacts.

People I'd helped, laughed with, lifted up, and shared rides and secrets with.

I called.

I texted.

I even sent voice notes I never thought I'd record.

"Bro, it's urgent. Just need to talk."

"Can you help me with a small push? I'll pay it back."

"Just need someone to hear me out…"

Do you know what I got in return?

Read. No reply.

Blue ticks. No voice.

"Will call you back." Never did.

Out of 2765 people,

less than 5 truly showed up.

The rest?

They ghosted.

Disappeared like smoke.

Vanished faster than a reel that flopped.

And I realized something brutal that day:

People love your light,

but they won't come looking when your battery dies.

The guys who used to call me "legend,"

The ones who copied my edits,

the ones who said "Anytime, bro" after every meetup—

were suddenly too busy, too broke, too quiet.

I wasn't angry.

Just… broken.

Because the world teaches you to build networks.

But life teaches you to value a handful of real ones.

And in that silence—

in that painful realization—

something inside me hardened.

Not into hate.

But into clarity.

I stopped calling.

Stopped begging.

Stopped chasing people who only showed up when the lights were on.

Because from that day forward,

I became my own backup.

My own rescue.

My own goddamn rider.

Chapter 19: Memory of Promises

They said it all once.

"Anytime you need me, I'm there."

"Bro, no matter what happens—we ride together."

"If life hits you, I'll be your helmet."

Back then, I believed every word.

Because when you're at the top—surrounded by noise, claps, and selfies—promises feel like tattoos. Permanent. Real. Unshakable.

But the truth?

They were just stickers.

Came off with a little rain.

The same boys who held my camera adjusted my angles, and hyped my edits—

now pretend like they never knew the password to my WiFi.

The ones who used to send voice notes full of "love you, bro"

don't even reply with a "take care" anymore.

But here's what hits hardest:

It's not that they forgot me.

It's that they forgot their own words.

I never asked for the moon.

Just for the same hand I once held out to them.

But when it was my turn to fall,

everyone had “things going on.”

And somehow, I became a burden.

The story they skip.

The message they leave unread.

I sat there, scrolling through chats—archived memories.

Laughing selfies.

Late-night pep talks.

Plans that never happened.

Dreams we built together that now feel like dust.

And as I stared at their promises,

I finally understood:

Some people don’t lie when they promise.

They just don’t know how to carry weight when it’s not their turn to shine.

I don’t hate them.

I’ve just stopped expecting them to show up.

Because promises are cheap.

But presence—that's rare.

And the next time someone says,

"I'm here for you,"

I'll smile politely…

And ride alone anyway.

Chapter 20: Loan Rejections & Lost Hope

When people disappear,

you don't stop dreaming.

You just try to find other ways to keep them alive.

For me, that meant walking into banks.

Wearing the best shirt I had left.

Carrying files of fake confidence.

Because all I wanted—was a small loan.

To breathe.

To build something again.

To show the world I wasn't finished.

I walked in with hope.

I walked out with rejection letters.

Each one is colder than the last.

"Low CIBIL score."

"Unstable income."

"Insufficient collateral."

"Not eligible."

They never looked at my story.

Only my numbers.

They didn't see the man who once inspired thousands.

Who helped others grow.

Who once had a garage full of dreams.

All they saw was a risk.

A failure.

A name that didn't match their definition of "potential."

One manager even said,

"Why don't you ask your followers for help, Mr. Influencer?"

I smiled.

Because I had already tried.

And all I got were "Thoughts & Prayers" in comment sections,

no cheques.

Loan after loan.

Attempt after attempt.

I started to realize something brutal:

You can be famous online,

but in real life, the system only respects balance sheets.

I came home that day.

Sat on my old bike.

Helmet on. Engine off.

And I just stayed there.

For hours.

Not crying. Not angry.

Just… hollow.

Because for the first time in years,

I had no idea what to do next.

The man who once rode at 300 km/h

was now scared to check his WhatsApp.

Hope didn’t vanish in a bang.

It died in pieces—with every rejected form,

every closed door,

every polite “sorry.”

And in that silence,

something inside me whispered:

“Maybe you were never meant to be helped.

Maybe you were meant to rebuild yourself.

Alone.”

Chapter 21: Natasha's Warmth

Rock bottom didn't echo with tears.

It echoed with her voice.

Just when I was done trying,

done trusting,

done picking up the pieces…

She texted.

"Hey, just checking in. You've been quiet. You okay?"

It wasn't a fancy message.

No poetry. No drama.

But it landed harder than all the fake "love you bros" ever had.

I typed a short reply:

"Yeah. Just tired."

But she didn't stop there.

"Want to talk? Or just… sit in silence on call?"

No one had ever offered me that before.

Silence.

Not advice.

Not solutions.

Just presence.

We got on a call.

And for the first few minutes, neither of us said much.

Just breathing.

Just existing.

Together.

And in that silence, I felt something strange—

Peace.

Like all the chaos in my head

had found a place to park for a while.

She didn't rush me.

She didn't pity me.

She just held space.

Over the next few days, her messages became the light I didn't know I needed.

"Drink water, dumbass."

"Go ride, even if it's just to the corner shop."

"You matter. Even when it doesn't feel like it."

Little things.

But when you're drowning,

even a straw feels like a life jacket.

And slowly,

without trying to be a saviour,

Natasha became my calm in the fire.

Not because she fixed anything.

But because she didn’t leave when I was broken.

She taught me that warmth isn’t in grand gestures.

It’s in consistency.

It’s in good mornings when you didn’t even reply last night.

It’s in asking how you are—and actually waiting for the answer.

And for the first time in a long time,

I wasn’t surviving for the next ride, or the next scheme, or the next shot at redemption.

I was living,

just to hear her voice again.

Chapter 22: Tea, Talk & Truth

We'd spoken for weeks.

Texted through late nights.

Shared silences that felt safer than most conversations I'd ever had.

But this was different.

This was the first meeting.

Not a date.

Not a setup.

Just two tired souls choosing to sit across from each other—with no expectations, no filters, and no noise.

We met at a small tea stall near the outskirts.

No cafés, no brand tags. Just mud cups cracked benches, and the kind of peace cities forget to offer.

She wore a simple kurti.

No makeup.

Hair tied in a loose bun.

I came in dusty jeans and an old riding jacket—because I didn't want to impress.

I wanted to be seen.

And she saw me.

Not the influencer.

Not the biker.

Just the man who had fallen and was still choosing to stand.

"You look tired," she said, stirring her tea.

"I've been carrying too much," I replied, not even pretending to smile.

That's how the conversation started.

Not with small talk.

But with truth.

We spoke about dreams that never came true.

Family pressure.

Loyalty that felt one-sided.

Death.

Trust.

Pain.

And hope that refused to die.

She told me about her own scars—hidden behind strong words and a calm voice.

We weren't flirting.

We weren’t planning.

We were just… healing.

One sip at a time.

One sentence at a time.

And when I said,

“I don’t know what I’m doing anymore.”

She simply said,

“That’s okay. You don’t have to know. You just have to keep showing up.”

No one had ever told me that before.

Not like this.

There was no hug.

No sparkly selfie.

But when I rode away that night, I realized something powerful:

Some people don’t enter your life to impress you.

They enter to remind you you’re human.

And that being human is enough.

Chapter 23: The Proposal Without a Ring

Where love doesn't come in grand gestures, but in quiet promises, shared dreams, and the hope of rebuilding together.

By now, Natasha wasn't just a name on my screen.

She was the first message I looked for in the morning,

and the last voice I wanted to hear before sleep.

It wasn't fast.

It wasn't dramatic.

It was… real.

After weeks of tea talks, shared rides, late-night laughs, and unspoken healing, something began to form between us.

Not sparks. Not butterflies.

But home.

One evening, we sat watching the city lights from a hillside.

No bikes. No noise.

Just us and the sound of the wind cutting through silence.

She leaned against my shoulder.

I looked at her, and I knew—this woman didn't fall in love with my reels, my rides, or my reputation.

She saw the man underneath the ashes.

The one who had lost everything but still dared to dream.

So I said it.

Not on one knee.

Not with a diamond.

Not with Instagram captions.

Just three words, wrapped in truth.

“Let’s build together.”

She looked at me—no shock, no drama—just that soft Natasha smile.

And she nodded.

“But no running away when it gets hard. No more silence. No more ego.”

“Deal,” I whispered.

That night, there were no fireworks.

Just the sound of two broken hearts quietly choosing each other over the world.

No ring.

No fancy dinner.

But in that moment, we were engaged in purpose.

In pain.

In potential.

It wasn't about a wedding.

It was about rebuilding from scratch—

this time, with someone who wouldn't walk away when the walls cracked again.

She didn't fix me.

But she held the blueprints to the new man I was becoming.

And that?

That meant more than any ceremony ever could.

Chapter 24: A Call at Midnight

We were getting closer.

Me and Natasha.

Conversations were deeper.

Smiles more frequently.

And for the first time in years, I was dreaming with someone—not alone.

Until that night.

It was past midnight.

I had just edited a video, sent it to her with a wink emoji, and was about to sleep.

The phone rang.

Natasha Calling.

Strange.

She never called this late.

I answered, joking,

"What, miss me already?"

But there was no laughter on the other end.

Only silence.

And breathing.

Then came three words that hit harder than any crash I'd ever had.

"I have cancer."

Time stopped.

The fan above me kept spinning.

The world kept moving.

But I… didn't.

I asked if she was joking.

She wasn't.

She said she had been feeling weak.

Went for a checkup.

The reports came back that day.

I sat on the floor.

My phone pressed against my ear like it was the only thing holding me up.

"Don't cry," she said.

"I'm not," I lied.

She was calm.

Too calm.

Maybe she hadn't processed it yet.

Or maybe she had accepted it faster than I could.

I wanted to scream.

To punch something.

To ride into the night and outrun the truth.

But instead, I just listened.

To her voice.

To her strength.

To the crack hiding inside her calmness.

She wasn't asking for sympathy.

She was preparing me.

"If I get weaker, promise me you won't stop your rides."

"Natasha…"

"Promise me you'll keep moving."

That night, I didn't sleep.

I stared at the ceiling,

remembering all the time's life hit me,

but this…

this was different.

This wasn't a failure.

This wasn't betrayal.

This was fate playing dirty.

And there was nothing I could do to stop it.

Chapter 25: Prayer & Denial

Cancer.

A six-letter word.

But it hits like a grenade.

Not just to the one who hears it, but to everyone who loves them.

Natasha didn’t fall apart.

So I did—quietly when she wasn’t looking.

She still smiled at our calls.

Still made fun of my bad jokes.

Still said “good night” like tomorrow was guaranteed.

But I knew.

I saw it in the slight delay in her words.

The tired eyes in our video calls.

The softness replaced her fire.

I wasn’t ready.

So I turned to something I hadn’t in a long time—

God.

Not out of devotion.

Out of desperation.

I lit candles.

Visited temples.

Went to churches.

Stood outside mosques.

Anywhere, everywhere.

"Please save her."

"Take anything from me, just not her."

"Let this be a mistake."

I whispered, begged, bargained.

And when the reports said "stage 2,"

I held onto it like it was a victory.

"We caught it early."

"There's hope."

"She's strong."

I started googling survivor stories.

Started planning diets.

Started believing that if I just loved her hard enough—she would live.

But in truth?

I was in denial.

Because no matter how brave she was,

no matter how strong we pretended to be—

the shadow of cancer was always sitting in the corner of every conversation.

Every time her message was late,

my heart raced.

Every time she said “I’m tired,”

I imagined the worst.

And still, I smiled in front of her.

Still said,

“You’ll be fine.”

“We’ll beat this.”

“I got you.”

But inside, I was a storm.

Of helplessness.

Of fear.

Of rage at the universe for giving me love… only to test me with loss.

I was fighting a battle with no sword, no shield, only faith.

And faith, sometimes, feels like sand slipping through your fingers.

Chapter 26: The Last Ride

She asked me quietly,

like it was just another day.

“Can we ride, one last time?”

Not go out.

Not hang out.

Not sit somewhere and talk.

Ride.

That word—it meant everything to us.

It was how we met.

How we bonded.

How we dreamed.

And now, how we would say goodbye—without saying a word.

I picked her up early morning.

Helmet on. Mask covering half her face.

Her eyes were already tired, but still shining.

I didn’t ask “Are you okay?”

I didn’t ask “Are you sure?”

Because I knew.

This wasn't for her health.

This was for her soul.

We took the coastal road.

Not fast.

Just steady.

Like every kilometre was a heartbeat she wanted to feel again.

She wrapped her arms around me.

No tight grip. Just enough to say—I'm here.

The wind felt different that day.

It wasn't rushing.

It was listening.

Even the sea beside us looked still like it understood the silence between us.

Halfway through, I slowed down.

"Want to stop?" I asked.

She shook her head.

"Not yet. Keep going."

So I did.

Past our favourite tea spot.

Past the cliff view.

Past every place that had once been a moment.

And when we finally did stop—

it wasn't planned.

She just tapped my shoulder gently.

I parked.

Took off my helmet.

Turned to her.

She didn't say anything.

Just removed her helmet, leaned her head on my back, and exhaled.

That sound—it wasn't just breath.

It was released.

Like she had emptied every fear into the wind and let the road carry it.

"Thank you," she whispered.

"For what?"

"For not treating me like I'm dying."

My chest tightened.

But I kept still.

Because this ride—this was for her.

Not for my grief.

Not for my fear.

Just… for her peace.

That was our last ride.

Not because we planned it that way.

But because life did.

Chapter 27: Smoke, Not Flame

I thought I was ready.

All those hospital visits, late-night prayers, fake smiles…

I thought I had prepared my heart.

But death doesn't knock.

It slides in through silence.

Through a phone that doesn't ring.

Through a text that never gets sent.

The morning it happened, the sky was grey.

No rain. No sun.

Just a heavy stillness—as if the universe knew something I didn't.

Then the call came.

Her sister.

Soft voice.

Breaking every word.

"She's gone…"

The room didn't spin.

It froze.

My breath paused.

Time didn't move.

I didn't move.

I just stared at the wall in front of me,

as if it would suddenly show her face

and say this was all some twisted joke.

But there was no punchline.

Only the empty echo of a love that wouldn't laugh again.

I rushed to the hospital.

Stood near her body.

Still. Peaceful. Too peaceful.

She looked like she was sleeping.

Like she might wake up and say,

"Chill, drama king. I'm fine."

But her fingers were cold.

And mine were shaking.

I wanted to scream.

To rage at God.

To punch the walls and break every mirror that showed me this wasn't a dream.

But I didn't.

I just sat beside her.

Held her hand.

And whispered everything I never got to say:

“I’m proud of you.”

“I’ll never forget the way you made silence feel safe.”

“You didn’t lose, Natasha. You just… rode ahead.”

And then I cried.

For real this time.

No one to hide from.

No one to protect.

Just me… and the ashes of a future we once dreamed together.

She left quietly.

No drama. No chaos.

Just smoke.

Not flame.

Not fire.

Just a soft, fading warmth that once was love—and always will be.

Chapter 28: The Silence After Goodbye

After the rituals, the condolences, the white flowers, and the crowd…

comes the most dangerous part of grief—silence.

No more calls.

No more updates.

No more "Let me know how she's doing."

Everyone goes back to their routines.

You're expected to go back to yours.

But what do you return to…

when your reason for waking up is gone?

I'd stare at her last message,

read it like scripture,

scrolling up, trying to feel the warmth behind her words.

Her number stayed in my favourites.

As if she'd text again.

I still typed "Good morning" some days.

Never sent it.

Just stared at it…

and deleted it.

The helmet she wore on our last ride stayed in the same place.

Untouched.

Like it still carried her scent.

Even the bike…

it felt heavier without her behind me.

Like it knew the ride was incomplete.

I stopped riding.

For weeks.

I couldn't hear the engine without hearing her laughter.

Couldn't cross that tea stall without feeling the phantom weight of her hand on my shoulder.

People said things like:

"Time heals."

"She's in a better place."

"Be strong."

But what they don't tell you is…

Time doesn't heal.

It just teaches you how to carry the weight without collapsing in public.

Her voice—gone.

Her scent—fading.

Her absence—louder than any crowd.

And the hardest part?

There's no final message.

No goodbye.

No closure.

Just this unending silence

that wraps around your chest like chains

and squeezes tighter with every memory.

She left without warning.

But left everything behind:

The love.

The lessons.

The pain.

The promise.

And that promise?

It's the only reason I didn't give up.

Chapter 29: Bedrest Diaries

After Natasha was gone, I kept trying to move like nothing had happened.

Smiling. Editing. Posting.

Pretending.

Running from the storm inside me.

But pain has a way of finding its way out.

And mine?

It came through my body.

First, it was just fatigue.

Then a fever.

Then my legs started giving out.

The doctor looked at me and said,

"You need rest. Not a day. Weeks. Maybe more."

My body had crashed.

Not because of sickness.

But because of grief, burnout, and silent war.

So, bed rest.

Me.

A rider.

A dreamer.

Now lying flat.

Watching ceilings. Counting fan blades.

And in that stillness… everything I'd buried came back.

Natasha's laughter in my ears.

Her last message blinked in my mind.

The broken business.

The betrayals.

Devika.

Mansoor.

Loss.

Rejection.

All of it flooded my chest like a dam that finally cracked.

No one came to visit.

Not the "Anytime bro" people.

Not the "Let's ride soon" folks.

Just me.

And the ghosts of the life I once thought I had control over.

I started writing.

Not for likes.

Not for a caption.

Just to survive.

Page after page, I poured everything out.

Tears.

Truth.

Rage.

Regret.

That notebook became my therapist.

My mirror.

My punching bag.

I wasn't riding the roads anymore.

I was riding memory lanes—

Some beautiful, most brutal.

But strangely…

that stillness started healing me.

Not fast.

Not fully.

But enough.

Enough to realize—

You can’t race away from pain.

You have to sit with it. Bleed with it.

And then… walk again.

Chapter 30: Real Friends, Real Silence

When life was loud—

when bikes roared,

stories trended,

and my smile fooled the world—

my phone never stopped ringing.

Hundreds of messages.

Riders tagging me.

Brands want me.

"Bro, you're killing it!"

"Next ride, I'm in!"

"You inspire me, man!"

But after Natasha's death…

after my body gave up…

after my world went quiet—

So did they.

2765 contacts.

2765 reminders that popularity doesn't mean presence.

In those long days of bedrest,

I waited.

For one message.

One call.

One knock at the door.

Silence.

The people I had cheered for, promoted, lifted, laughed with—

gone.

And that's when it hit me:

They weren't friends.

They were fans.

Friends don't disappear when the camera turns off.

Real ones show up without needing a caption.

And to be honest…

it hurt more than the illness.

More than the betrayal.

Because I had believed—genuinely believed—that these people loved me.

Turns out, they loved the version of me that was winning.

Not the broken man.

Not the grieving soul.

Not the quiet, jobless, dreamless me.

Just the rider with reach.

But amid that silence…

a few voices stayed.

Not many.

But real ones.

The kind who sent food without asking.

The kind who checked on me at 2 AM when they couldn't sleep either.

The kind who said,

"Don't worry about talking, I'll just sit on the call so you don't feel alone."

They didn't need words.

They didn't need a reason.

They just showed up.

And those few?

They were enough.

Chapter 31: The Shadow on My Wall

It starts with small things.

You stop opening the curtains.

You forget what day it is.

You hear the fan hum and realize—it's the only sound in your life now.

The light outside means nothing.

Because inside, everything is dark.

I used to race time.

Now I just watched it.

Tick. Tick. Tick.

Mocking me.

I lay there, staring at the wall.

And on that wall—

a shadow.

Mine. But not really.

It looked like me.

But felt like something else.

A reflection of the person I had become:

Still breathing,

but not alive.

I'd talk to it sometimes.

Out loud.

Like a madman.

"You happy now?"

"This is what you wanted, right?"

"She's gone. They're gone. I'm done."

Some nights, the thoughts would get louder.

What's the point?

Why live like this?

Who even cares if you disappear?

That shadow—it never answered.

Just stared back.

Silent. Cold. Familiar.

Loneliness wasn't just in my room.

It was under my skin.

In my breath.

On the way, even my dreams stopped visiting.

No bikes.

No vlogs.

No plans.

Just one man, a broken past, and a shadow on a peeling wall.

But maybe that was the point.

To be stripped of everything.

To be emptied.

So that something new—something real—could be built again.

Rock bottom doesn't feel like a crash.

It feels like silence that stretches forever.

But deep in that silence…

a voice whispers:

"You're still here."

"You're not done."

Chapter 32: The Man in the Mirror

One morning—after weeks of silence, sickness, and sleepless nights—

I stood up.

Not because I felt better.

But because I had to see.

I dragged myself to the mirror.

Looked straight into the eyes of a man I didn't recognize anymore.

Sunken cheeks.

Unshaved.

Eyes tired, red, almost hollow.

But beyond the face…

I saw something else.

Weight.

Not physical.

Emotional.

Spiritual.

I saw the weight of dreams lost.

Of love buried.

Of friends vanished.

Of businesses burned.

Of engines silenced.

That mirror didn't lie.

It showed me the truth I had avoided for months:

I was not okay.

But it also showed me something else—

I was still standing.

Barely.

Weakly.

But standing.

And in that moment, I realized—

this man in the mirror…

he wasn't finished.

He was forged.

Every betrayal,

every breakdown,

every death,

every downfall—

Had melted me, bent me, shattered me…

But didn't erase me.

Not yet.

So I stared at that broken reflection and said:

"You've lost everything…

But you still have you."

"And that's enough to start."

Chapter 33: The Road Ahead

It didn't start with a roar.

Not with a motivational playlist or some dramatic comeback.

It started with one small decision:

Get up.

Not for Instagram.

Not to prove anyone wrong.

Not even to feel better.

Just to take back one inch of the man I used to be.

I tied my shoes—shaking hands.

Opened the door—sunlight hit like a slap and a blessing.

Stepped outside—no destination, just direction.

The world hadn't changed.

Same roads.

Same buildings.

Same strangers.

But I had.

I wasn't chasing fame anymore.

I wasn't addicted to likes, applause, or approval.

I just wanted peace.

Purpose.

A ride with meaning—not mileage.

So I made a plan.

Simple. Small. Real.

Eat better.

Walk every day.

Speak to my parents—not about goals, just about life.

Write what I felt, not what people wanted to hear.

And yes… one day—ride again.

But this time, not to escape.

To return.

To everything I once loved… on my terms.

The road ahead wasn't smooth.

It wasn't even fully visible.

But I knew one thing:

I'd burned.

I'd crashed.

I'd lost.

But I hadn't quit.

Because inside the ashes—

something still flickered.

A spark.

And that was enough.

Chapter 34: The Call That Changed Nothing

The room was quiet. Too quiet. The kind of silence that didn't comfort—it pressed against your chest, reminded you how alone you really were.

I was sitting on my old plastic chair, scrolling through nothing on my phone, mind already heavy with the weight of unpaid bills, broken dreams, and the unbearable silence of people who once promised forever.

And then, my phone rang.

Kuruvila.

A name I hadn't heard in a while, but one that didn't bring any bad memories. Not yet. He'd always seemed genuine—helpful, kind, a bit too talkative maybe—but in a world full of masks, he wore his well. Still, something about his voice this time had an urgency to it. Like he wasn't just calling to check in—he had something to offer.

A business proposal, he said.

Film industry.

I laughed—dry, tired, honest. I told him straight: "Bro, I don't have money for this. I'm already burning."

But he didn't back off. He talked like this was fate—like this could be the last shot to crawl out of the mess I was in.

He said, “This is not an investment, it’s support. The film is already 50% done. The producer is on the edge—no funds, and suicidal thoughts. Just a push. Three months. You’ll get it all back, with a bonus.”

It wasn’t my problem. I knew that.

But pain does something strange—it makes you believe in hope, even when it comes dressed in desperation.

I talked to Jacob. Thaju was like me—new to all this movie stuff but with dreams bigger than his bank account. He listened, nodded, and asked the right questions. He didn’t say no. That was all Kuruvila needed.

Soon, the three of us—me, Kuruvila, and Thaju—sat across from the man who started it all: Joseph, the film producer.

He spoke with emotion, with stories, with tears waiting to fall. He promised everything:

“We just need support. We’ll handle the rest. Whether the movie hits or flops, we’ll return every rupee—with a gift. Within 15 days of release. Promise.”

I don’t know if it was his words or my own desperation that won.

But we gave the money.

And waited.

One week passed.

One month.

Six months.

A year.

Three years.

No money. No calls. No answers. Just silence.

What started as a promise turned into a betrayal. What felt like brotherhood became another scar.

I wasn't even sure if Kuruvila knew. Or if he was part of it. His behaviour was always good—but now, even that felt rehearsed. Or maybe I just didn't know how to trust anymore.

The silence turned into anger.

The anger turned into action.

And so, the legal war began.

Chapter 35: Truth in Black and White

The first time I stood in the lawyer's office, I felt like I was walking into a battlefield with no armour.

I had no background in legal stuff, and no idea how this world worked. But I had two things—documents and pain. Enough to start a war.

We filed the case.

Fraud. Breach of contract. Mental harassment.

The papers didn't lie, but people? People do.

Kuruvila stopped answering my calls. The same guy who once spoke to me like a brother, who told me this would be our "comeback," disappeared. I didn't know if he was scared, guilty, or just playing his role from the beginning. That mystery hurt more than the money itself.

Jacob stood by me for a while—silent, supportive. But as the months dragged on and the court dates got delayed, even he started to fade. People say time reveals everything. For me, it revealed how alone a man can be when there's nothing left to offer.

In court, they acted like we never existed.

Joseph claimed he never promised repayment. That there was no agreement. That it was "support," not business.

I remembered every word he said, every emotional line. But in court, it's not about memory—it's about proof.

We submitted everything.

Voice recordings. Messages. WhatsApp chats. Bank transactions.

Still, the system moved slowly—slower than healing.

I started losing sleep. Not because of the money—but the betrayal.

The film? It got released.

Did decent in a few theatres.

And yet, not a rupee came back.

That's when I realized—some people don't cheat you for money.

They cheat you because they can.

Because you trusted them.

I began questioning everything.

Was I a fool? Was I used?

Or was this all just another test from life, burning away the fake ones before the final chapter?

Chapter 36: Born of Ash

One of those nights, when everything felt heavy and hopeless, I sat on my bed in the dark—no music, no noise, no fake motivation. Just silence.

And in that silence, her voice came back to me.

Natasha.

The one I had lost to time, to choices, to fate.

I don't know why I thought of her then.

Maybe because she was the last person who truly saw me—not as a rider, not as a fighter, not as a brand. Just… me.

She had a way of saying things that hit deeper than any quote or motivational reel. And at that moment, I remembered her words.

"You fall, you rise. You break, you heal. Just don't stop being you, Shiva. Even if the world turns its back—don't you ever turn your back on yourself."

I closed my eyes and held on to that.

It wasn't a phone call.

It wasn't real-time support.

But it was enough.

Her words stitched something back in me.

Maybe not the whole heart. But enough to make it beat again.

So I stood up.

Washed my face.

And pulled out my riding jacket.

Because I knew—if she believed in me then, I could believe in me now.

Chapter 37: Ashes Don't Lie

I stopped waiting for justice.

The court dates stretched endlessly, like a bad dream that refused to end. Lawyers switched, excuses multiplied, and slowly, everyone involved began vanishing like smoke. Even the anger started to dry up.

What was left? Just… me.

Me, and the ashes.

I looked around at what I'd become—burnt out, broken, betrayed. I had trusted people with my dreams, my heart, my name. And all I got in return was silence and court papers.

But there's something strangely pure about hitting the bottom.

Because when you lose everything, you also lose the fear of losing.

That's when it started.

The rebirth.

No big speeches. No inspirational quotes. Just small things.

Waking up early. Riding again—not for reels or likes, but for me.

I pulled my old GoPro from the shelf. Dusted off the helmet.

Started recording again.

Not to impress.

Not to prove.

Just to tell my story.

Every ride became therapy. Every vlog is a release. And slowly, without realizing it, people started watching again. But this time, I didn't care if they did or didn't. The fire was mine now. Not for fame. Not for followers. For me.

I rebuilt alone.

No sponsors. No investors. No fake friends.

And in that loneliness, I found something I'd lost years ago—peace.

Chapter 38: Fire Doesn't Destroy, It Reveals

It took me years to understand: that life doesn't betray you.

People do.

But if you survive that betrayal, if you stand in the fire long enough without letting it consume you—

You come out forged.

Stronger.

Sharper.

Free.

The film money never came back. The court case is still stuck in the cracks of the system.

But I stopped checking the updates.

Because I started writing a new script. One where I am the creator.

Not a film.

Not a business.

But a life.

My story.

And this is where The Man Who Rode Through Fire ends—not with revenge, not with a win in court, but with a man who walked out of flames with scars… and a purpose.

The ride continues.

But this time, I ride for no one else—

Only for the man in the mirror.

Chapter 39: Truth in Black and White

Months after the legal case was filed, silence from Joseph was expected. Kuruvila's disappearance hurt. But what I never saw coming… was Jacob turning against me.

One evening, out of nowhere, my phone lit up.

Jacob.

I thought maybe he had some update, maybe he wanted to stand together and face this as brothers. But the voice that came through wasn't the friend I knew. It wasn't supported. It was pressure.

"Shiva… if they don't return the money, YOU have to give me my share back. I trusted YOU. You made me meet them. If I don't get it back, you'll have to deal with me."

I stayed silent for a second. Not because I didn't have anything to say. But because my heart had taken one more unexpected hit.

I reminded him—I lost more than him. I was the one who spoke to Kuruvila. I was the one who believed. I stood beside him not as a middleman but as someone who walked into this together.

But none of it mattered.

He didn't want the truth. He wanted someone to blame.

And in the end, it was easier to turn on me than to fight the real problem.

Calls like that kept coming—sometimes angry, sometimes silent, sometimes with a tone that felt more like a threat than a conversation. I could feel it… the thread of trust snapping in slow motion.

And just like that, the last person I thought I could trust became another shadow.

It wasn't just betrayal anymore. It was isolation.

And it cut deeper than any lie.

Chapter 40: The Last Flame Falls

When Jacob turned on me, something inside finally broke.

It wasn't just the words—"You brought me into this. If they don't pay, you will."

It was the fact that even someone who stood shoulder to shoulder with me now saw me as the problem, not the victim.

And that was the final burn. Not from strangers. Not from enemies. But from someone I once called brother.

I stopped picking up his calls.

Not because I was afraid.

But because there was nothing left to say.

I had nothing to return—no money, no friendship, no trust.

Only pain.

And it wasn't shareable anymore.

I sat alone one night—helmet beside me, jacket thrown on the floor, silence screaming in the room—and I asked myself a simple question:

"What's left of me now?"

The answer was quiet, but clear:

Me.

I decided that night—I wouldn't chase answers anymore.

I wouldn't wait for apologies that would never come, or justice that moved too slow.

Let the law run its course. Let karma do its job.

I had something more important to do.

Rebuild.

I sold what I could. Cleared my space. Deleted numbers. I unfollowed everyone who reminded me of the fall.

Then I pulled out my old riding gloves, and with them, I picked up the only thing that ever made sense—the ride.

I started recording again.

But this time, it wasn't for reels. It wasn't too trendy.

It was for the truth.

My truth.

Vlogs turned into stories. Stories turned into messages. And people started writing back.

Not sponsors. Not opportunists.

Real people.

People who'd been cheated.

People who'd been left behind.

People who burned too—but never stopped riding.

And slowly… something strange happened.

I didn't get rich. I didn't go viral.

But I got peace.

The real kind. The kind that doesn't come from likes views or promises.

It comes from knowing you survived—without becoming like them.

"The Man Who Rode Through Fire"

I still wear the scars.

I still ride with memories of voices that once promised forever and left at the first sign of trouble.

But I also ride with something more powerful—truth.

I was broken. Betrayed. Cheated. Threatened. Forgotten.

But I never stopped riding.

And I never lost me.

If this story reaches even one soul who's been through the same—who trusted the wrong ones, who gave their heart to liars, who invested in dreams that turned to dust—

Let this be your reminder:

You can burn and still rise.

You can fall and still ride.

You can lose everything… and still find yourself.

This isn't the story of a hero.

This is the story of a man who rode through fire—

And lived to tell it.

9 789356 056664

Printed at Repro India Ltd.